Rocket Boy

by Damon Lehrer

David R. Godine · *Publisher* · Boston

To my family.
–DL

First published in 2017 by
David R. Godine, Publisher
Post Office Box 450
Jaffrey, New Hampshire 03452
www.godine.com

Library of Congress Cataloging-in-Publication Data

Names: Lehrer, Damon, author, illustrator.
Title: Rocket boy / by Damon Lehrer.
Description: Jaffrey, New Hampshire : David R. Godine, 2016. |
Summary: Armed only with a pencil and a pad of paper, a boy
transports himself into adventures where he meets new friends, visits
unseen landscapes, and makes his way back to his own bed before dawn.
Identifiers: LCCN 2016022973 | ISBN 9781567925876 (alk. paper)
Subjects: | CYAC: Imagination--Fiction. | Drawing--Fiction. |
Stories without words.
Classification: LCC PZ7.1.L4438 Ro 2016 | DDC [E]--dc23
LC record available at https://lccn.loc.gov/2016022973

First edition
Printed in Canada

1

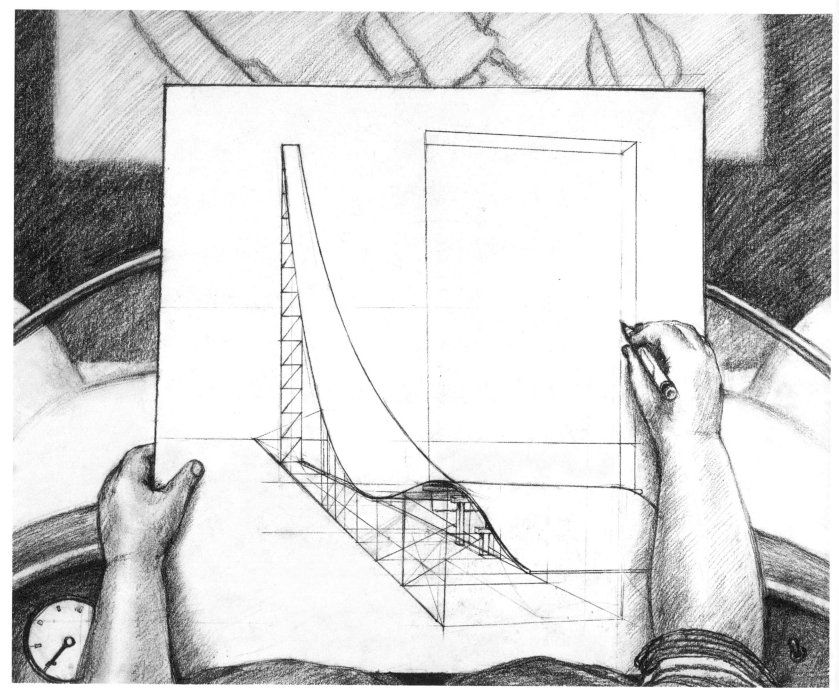

15

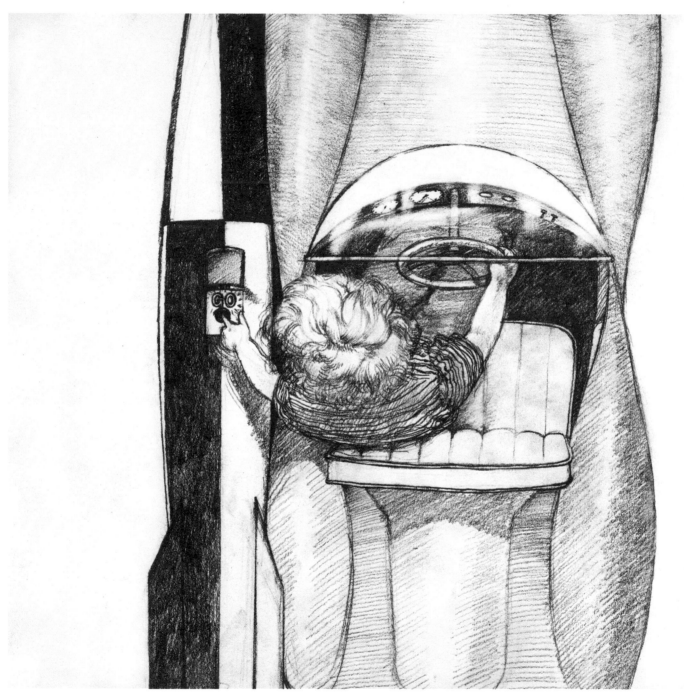

26

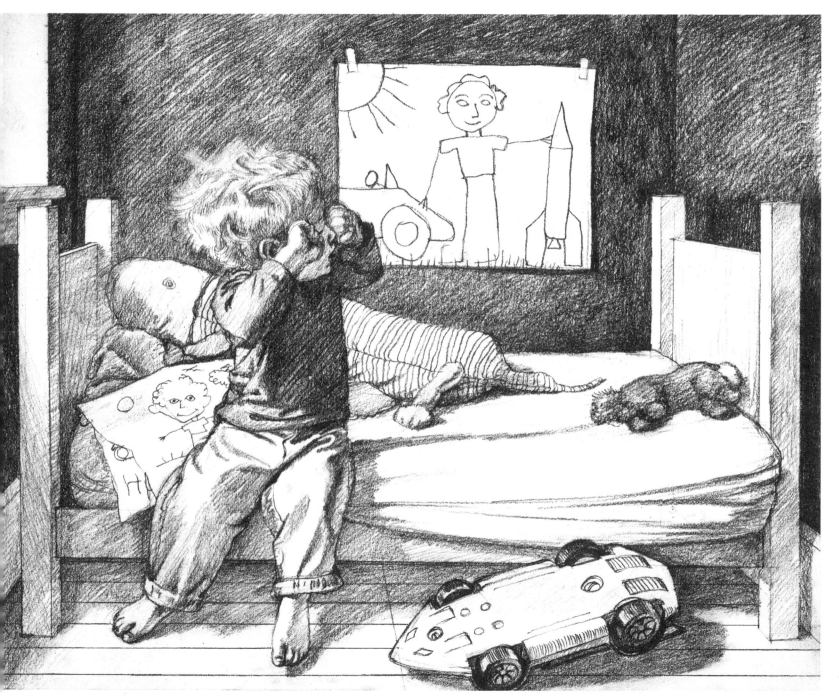